Fi
or

CW00858380

Image Copyright Ⓒhamishfoundation.co.uk

**Proceeds from the sale of this book will benefit
The Hamish Foundation of St. Andrews.**

Two Herons
Studio

www.robertheron.net

**Hamish McHamish,
the famous St. Andrews cat,
was having a wee catnap.
He was dreaming of a fish in a bowl.**

When Hamish awoke, he decided to go for a walk along the beautiful St. Andrews beach. In the distance, a large fishing boat was lifting its net full of fish from the sea.

**But, caught in the large net was a mermaid.
Her name was Morag the Mermaid, and
she had a broken tail fin.
"Please, help me!" Morag called out.**

**Sammy seagull flew to Hamish and said,
"Morag the Mermaid needs help.
She has a broken tail fin."
"Okay, Sammy. I'll get her an ambulance."**

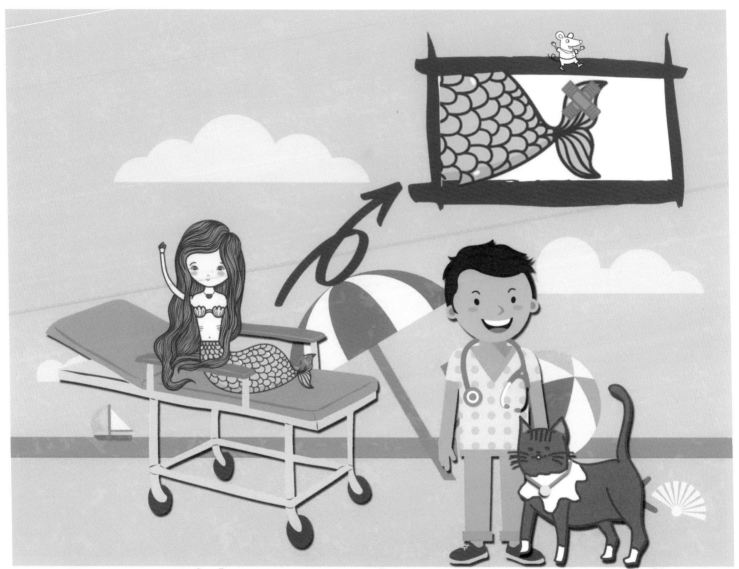

Doctor Dick put two plasters on Morag's fin and said, "Thanks, Hamish, for calling the ambulance. I'll take her to the aquarium." Morag smiled and waved at Hamish.

From all over Scotland, children brought their parents to see Morag the Mermaid, with the broken fin. The St. Andrews Aquarium was filled to overflowing every day.

"Please can I have plasters on my
shoe just like Morag the Mermaid?" asked
little Loulou sitting on her dad's shoulders.
"Hamish said I could if I asked real nice!"
"Me too!" "And me!" said all the other children.

Soon, all over St. Andrews, shoes of all different types had two plasters attached in solidarity with Morag the Mermaid. Flip-flops, baby shoes, even ballerina flats.

**All the newspapers were telling the story
of Morag the Mermaid and her broken fin.
Children all over Scotland now
had plasters put on their shoes.**

Hamish visited Morag every day, telling her about how famous she was.
"But, I want to go home, Hamish. I miss my friends under the sea. I'm sad," said Morag.

**Hamish asked Daisy Donkey to help
pull Morag from the aquarium
to the sea. She sat on a beach wheelchair.
"This is so much fun," said Morag.**

"Hamish, come for a swim with me."
Little Archie was fishing and said,
"You can use my scuba kit if you want!"
Hamish smiled and said, "Thank you, Archie!"

"Follow me to the bottom of the sea," said
Morag the Mermaid.
"Can I see your house?" asked Hamish.
"It's not a house. It's a castle!"

"What is a school bus doing under the sea?" asked Hamish. "Mermaid children go to school here. They learn their A-B-C's just like all children!"

"Thank you so much for showing me your beautiful castle," said Hamish. "Perhaps one day you will have your very own castle," said Morag the Mermaid.

Next day, Hamish sat outside the Pet Shop wondering how he could buy a Fish Bowl and a pet fish. Something to remind him of beautiful, Morag the Mermaid.

**Hamish loved the big aquarium.
He sat for hours and hours watching the
fish swim and swim around.
"Maybe one day," said Hamish.**

Hamish took a walk to St. Andrews University to meet some friends and tell them about wanting an aquarium.
"Where will you keep it?" asked Daisy.
"In the pet shop," said Hamish.

And soon all the town's cats and dogs
were telling their owners about Hamish
wanting his very own aquarium.
"We all love Hamish. We should do something."

All the St. Andrews mums and dads and children ran a 5K to raise funds for both the town's aquarium (for helping Morag the Mermaid), and for Hamish's very own aquarium.

And soon Hamish was given the aquarium by the town for helping Morag the Mermaid, and for encouraging the children to make her feel at home. He even had his very own castle. Hamish McHamish was very happy.

-The End-

Hamish McHamish

St Andrews *Beach* WHEELCHAIRS

Donations are always welcome and we have a 'Just Giving' page.

hamishfoundation.co.uk

If you have any ideas for fundraising or wish to volunteer to help us with the Foundation then please contact: hello@hamishfoundation.co.uk

Also by R.L.Heron

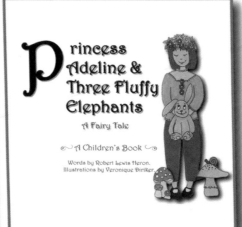

Also by Two Herons Studio

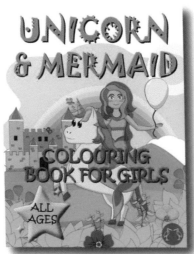

Printed in Great Britain
by Amazon